Blue Cheese Breath
and Stinky Feet

Published by
MAGINATION PRESS
An Educational Publishing Foundation Book
American Psychological Association
750 First Street, NE
Washington, DC 20002

For more information about our books, including a complete catalog, please write to us,
call 1-800-374-2721, or visit our website at www.maginationpress.com.

Editor: Darcie Conner Johnston
Art Director: Susan K. White
The text type is Versailles
Printed by Phoenix Color

Library of Congress Cataloging-in-Publication Data

DePino, Catherine.
Blue cheese breath and stinky feet : how to deal with bullies / written by Catherine DePino ;
illustrated by Bonnie Matthews.
p. cm.
Summary: With his parents' help, Steve devises an eleven-point plan to deal with the school bully.
ISBN 1-59147-111-7 (alk. paper) — ISBN 1-59147-112-5 (pbk. : alk. paper)
[1. Bullies—Fiction.] I. Matthews, Bonnie, 1963- ill. II. Title.
PZ7.D4395Bl 2004
[Fic]—dc22   2003020676

Manufactured in the United States of America
10 9 8 7 6 5 4 3 2 1

Blue Cheese Breath and Stinky Feet

HOW TO DEAL WITH BULLIES

written by Catherine DePino, Ed.D.

illustrated by Bonnie Matthews
and Charles Beyl

MAGINATION PRESS•WASHINGTON, DC

DEAR READER,

At one time or another, most of us have had to deal with teasing, people saying mean things about us, or others even trying to harm us. As a teacher, I've seen many kids hurt by bullying—both the emotional kind and the physical.

It can be hard to feel good about yourself when somebody's making fun of you or threatening you. You might worry that you deserve it, or that people think you're weak, or that you'll get teased or rejected by others if you tell someone. You might be afraid that you're in physical danger. The pain is hard to take, but you don't want to give the bully a reason to hurt you more. You feel alone and don't know where to go for help. What do you do?

In *Blue Cheese Breath and Stinky Feet,* Steve knows he needs to do something about Gus. But he doesn't want the other kids to think he's a baby or a tattletale, and he doesn't want to make things worse for himself with Gus. He is at the end of his rope.

In this story, a teacher calls Steve's parents and tells them about the problem. He had dreaded his parents finding out, but to his surprise, he feels better now that his parents know. Confiding in your parents or another trusted adult can often bring a sense of both relief and safety—a sense that things can get better, it's not your fault, people care about you, and you'll get the help you need to deal with the bully. The other good news Steve learns is that no matter what happens and no matter how bad things seem, you can always do something to help yourself. And that is exactly what Steve does. He and his parents think up and practice almost a dozen different things he can do to stop the bullying. They call it The Plan.

The Plan can work for you too. It contains lots of strategies for avoiding, defending against, and disarming any kind of bully. Learn the strategies of The Plan and practice them with your parents or other family members or friends. You can even practice by yourself in front of the mirror—or your dog or cat! Don't be discouraged if your efforts don't work the first time. It may take a few tries for the bully to realize that you're not a good target. Keep in mind that most things don't change overnight, but they will if you stick with it. The more you practice and use the strategies, the more confident you'll become, the less afraid you will feel, and the easier it will be to remember what to do when the time comes. And always remember, you are not alone.

I wish you peace!
Catherine DePino

Contents

CHAPTER 1

Mean Green Eyes

Gus jumped in front of me when I got off the bus.

He was thin as spaghetti, thinner than me.

But he had mean green eyes and a nasty laugh that stung like a hornet.

He moved up close and yelled in my face, "You have blue cheese breath and stinky feet!"

Some kids in my class laughed.

I ran home faster than a wild pony,
stomped up to my room,
and slammed the door.

I beat my fists on the wall like a drum.

"What's wrong?" Mom asked.

"Nothing," I said.

"Your face looks as gray as a cloudy day.
Did you fail a test?
Get in trouble at school?"

What would Gus do if I told?
No way, I can't take the chance.

"Nothing like that," I said.
"Is it okay if I go to Drew's?"

"Sure, but if you want to talk,
I'm here."

CHAPTER 2

Bad to Worse

The next day Gus tripped me in the hall. He pointed at me and laughed.

"Blue Cheese Breath and Stinky Feet, your mama eats cow brains."

A couple of Gus's creepy friends closed in like crows. They laughed loud and long.

My teacher Ms. Ruiz helped me up.
"Are you okay? What happened here?"

"I'm fine. I must have tripped."

"Go to class," she told Gus and his friends.

"Haw haw," they squawked as they
walked by.

I'd like to tell her.
But what if Gus finds out?

Later Gus caught up with me
in the lunch line.

He scrunched up his mean green eyes.
"Give me your money, or you'll be sorry."

"I don't think so," I said in a small,
scared voice.

He walked away laughing, like he
was king of the universe.

"Don't listen to him,"
said my friend Drew.
"He's all talk."

I could feel my
stomach doing flip-flops.
"That's easy for you
to say."

When I got on the bus, Gus slithered up to my seat. His toady friend held me down. They tickled my ribs.

The bus driver shouted, "Knock it off or I'll stop this bus."

"I told you you'd be sorry," Gus hissed and slithered back to his seat.

Don't cry. Don't cry.
If I cry I might as well die.

I jumped off the bus and ran home
as fast as I could.

I felt like a firecracker ready to go off.

But my knees were shaking and my
mouth tasted like I swallowed chalk.

That night at dinner Dad looked in my eyes. "What's wrong, Son?"

"Why do you think something's wrong?"

Dad pointed at my dessert.
"For one thing, your ice cream's a mushy mess. Fluffernutter Fudge is your favorite flavor."

"May I be excused? I need to do my homework."

"I think something's going on," said Dad. "I'd like to help. If you'll let me."

What if he thinks it's my fault?

What if he thinks I'm a crybaby?

What if he thinks I should be able to make Gus stop?

"It's really nothing, Dad," I said.

Dead Meat

The next morning Gus sneaked up to my seat from the back of the bus.

He tapped my shoulder hard. "Hand over your homework. I want to copy it."

"No way," I said. But my voice didn't match my words.

I dug in my backpack for my homework. Gus yanked it out of my hand.

Drew and Matt were sitting across
the aisle. They frowned.

"You don't have to take that from him,"
said Drew.

"Don't give in," said Matt.

I could feel Gus's hot, heavy breath
on my neck.

Drew and Matt looked at each other
and then at me.

"I see what you mean," Drew said.

"Not a guy to mess with," said Matt.

At lunch, Ms. Ruiz said, "Let's talk."

I sat down and stared at my shoes.

She fished a crumpled paper from her purse. "I found this on the floor: 'Beware. You can't escape the Mighty Me, Blue Cheese Breath and Stinky Feet. Hee hee.'"

My teacher's eyes looked dark and sad.
"I also saw you fall in the hall."

If only I could tell her.

I bet she'd understand.

But what will happen if I do?

Will things get even worse?

Gus was watching me and Ms. Ruiz.

The bell rang, and I made for the door like a rocket.

I'm dead meat.

After lunch Gus wrote me a note.

My heart pounded like a galloping stallion.
My stomach grumbled and growled.

Should I tell?

Will all the kids think I'm a tattletale?

Will they hate me?

Will I have any friends?

CHAPTER 4

The Plan

That night Mom said, "Your teacher called. She said that someone's been bothering you."

Dad said, "Now we know why you didn't want to talk or play."

"I won't tell. I can't," I said. "But I have to do something to make Gus stop. I can't take it anymore."

"There's a lot you can do, Son," said Dad.

Mom said, "Let's practice the things you can say and do to make this Gus stop bothering you."

Dad said, "We'll call it The Plan."

I breathed out a big whoosh of air.

I felt like somebody had lifted a barbell from my chest.

"You know, Son, guys like Gus aren't as big and bad as you think. And if you don't play their game, sometimes they give up and go away. So for starters, try to avoid Gus as much as you can."

"You mean move to another planet?" I asked. "He's always around."

Dad smiled. "Just try to fly under his radar if you can."

"I can also try ignoring him
if he starts up with me.

I'll pretend he's a harmless flea."

"You can also make it a point to stay
with friends," Mom said.
"He'll be less likely to bug you then."

"I'll talk to Drew and Matt," I said. "He
scares them too, but I know they'll help."

Suddenly, I thought of something.

What if these things don't work?
What do I do then?

CHAPTER 5

What If?

Dad must have read my mind.

"It helps to stand up straight and tall," he said.

"And it wouldn't hurt to look up and not down," said Mom.

I threw out my chest and looked up toward the sky. "I'm starting to feel the power now."

"That's it," said Dad. "Feel your strength. Tell yourself you're strong. And try not to let him know he's getting to you."

"What can you say to show Gus you
mean business?" Mom asked.

I flexed my muscle. "I'll use power words.
Like *I need you to move* instead of
Will you please move?"

"Now you're cooking," said Dad,
"short statements instead of questions."

33

"And here's the power word of all power words," said Mom. "*Gus*. Call the bully by his name."

A light bulb went on in my head. "But no insults. And no teasing."

Dad put his thumbs up. "You've got it, Son."

"Laughing is good, though. I can make a joke, without making fun."

"That's right," said Dad. "And if he still gets in your face, you can shout so other people can hear you."

"Ready to practice The Plan?" Dad asked.

"Let's do it," I said.

Dad shook his fist in front of my nose.

"Out of my way or I'll smash you to bits," he roared.

I stood up straight and looked up, not down.

"I need you to leave me alone, Cornelius," I said.

"That's my name," said Dad, laughing.

Now Mom's turn. She slapped her hands on her waist and scowled.

"Want to get past me? You'll have to move me first."

I grabbed a paper towel tube and shouted into it, "Help! SOS! Mayday! Call 9-1-1! Call in the troops, General Washington!"

Why not go all the way?

"And if you don't go away, Gus, I'm calling Ms. Ruiz."

CHAPTER 6

Check

The next afternoon, we marched to gym. Gus and one of his friends caught up with me.

Oh boy, here we go.

The Plan played through my brain like a movie:

THE PLAN

KEEP AWAY.

IGNORE THE BULLY.

STAY WITH FRIENDS.

STAND UP STRAIGHT AND TALL.

LOOK UP, NOT DOWN.

BE STRONG.

USE POWER WORDS.

MAKE A JOKE, BUT DON'T MAKE FUN.

SHOUT SO OTHERS WILL HEAR.

TELL A TEACHER OR COUNSELOR.

Gus nudged his friend. "Want to meet
someone with blue cheese breath
and stinky feet?"

His friend shrugged.

I looked into Gus's mean green eyes.

LOOK UP, NOT DOWN—check.

STAND UP STRAIGHT AND TALL—check.

"I'd like to meet him, too," I said.

MAKE A JOKE—check.

Gus's friend frowned at him.
"He doesn't seem scared to me."

"We'll see," Gus said. "We'll see."

Later that day, at the water fountain, Gus thumped me like a tom tom on the back.

"Stop that!" I said in a voice as loud as a police siren. "I am not a punching bag."

USE POWER WORDS—check.

SHOUT SO OTHERS WILL HEAR—check.

The teacher on recess duty shook his finger at Gus. "Keep your hands to yourself, young man."

"Yes, sir," he said in a syrupy voice.

"I'll get you later," Gus whispered.

"We'll see, Gus," I said.

BE STRONG.

CALL THE BULLY BY NAME.

Check, check.

Next period, Ms.Ruiz said,
"Clear your desks. Time for a quiz."

Gus passed me a note:
"Give me the answers, or I'll get you
after school."

BE STRONG popped into my brain again.
I ripped the note in two.

"You're dead," he said. "You're dead."

Was I in over my head?

CHAPTER 7

No Going Back

The bell rang. Time to go home.
I saw Gus hiding behind the door.

He jumped out at me like a green-eyed tiger.
"Ready to fight?"

No going back.

This is not going to be easy.

But I can do it.

I threw out my chest, stood strong and
tall, and looked straight into Gus's eyes.
I shouted over the noise of lockers
slamming and the principal calling busses
over the PA.

"Gus, I need you to go away.
I don't want to fight."

Drew, Matt, and some other friends
had gathered by the door.

"Way to go, Steve!" they called.

Gus stared at me with his green eyes.
His lips curled in a sneer, but somehow he
didn't seem scary, mean, or quite as tall.

"What's gotten into you, Blue Cheese
Breath? You aren't thinking straight at all."

POWER WORDS came to my rescue again.

"My name is Steve," I said.
"I need you to leave."

My friends cheered.

My teacher stood outside her room,
watching.

Gus glanced at her and muttered,
"I'm not getting in trouble
for old Stinky Feet."

As Gus slipped out
the door, I heard
him say, " Blue
Cheese Breath and
Stinky Feet, I'll get
you another day."

"Never again," I said. "No way."

Gus didn't follow me home that day.
Instead, he turned and walked away.

Drew and Matt gave me a double
high five.

Hooray, Hooray.

"Dad, Mom! The Plan worked great!
It wasn't as hard as I thought.
No black eyes or broken bones.
And I think Gus is going to leave me alone."

"This calls for a celebration," said Mom.

"We'll make a special dinner," said Dad.

"I could eat every taco in Mexico!
But there's one thing I need to know."

"Blue cheese.
What does blue cheese smell like?"

Dad laughed. "Want to try some
in your salad?"

"No," I said. "I think I'd rather have
pepperoni pizza and Fluffernutter Fudge
ice cream, if that's okay with you."

Someday I might try blue cheese.

But not for a long, long time.

Maybe never.

ABOUT THE AUTHOR

CATHERINE DEPINO, Ed.D., has had years of hands-on experience with bullies and the bullied through her work as a high school teacher and student disciplinarian in the Philadelphia school system. Her daughter Shayna, a school guidance counselor, encouraged her to write *Blue Cheese Breath and Stinky Feet* to help children of all ages with this persistent and painful challenge. Dr. DePino has three daughters and three grandchildren—Drew, Hope, and Luke. She lives in Bucks County, Pennsylvania, with her husband, Andrew, a retired teacher.

Acknowledgments: My deepest thanks to Darcie Johnston, an expert editor who takes the time to listen and understand. Thanks also to Mary Louise Roberts, librarian at the Bucks County Peace Center. — CD

ABOUT THE ILLUSTRATORS

BONNIE MATTHEWS has illustrated many children's books. In addition, her whimsical characters have appeared in more than 100 magazines worldwide, and on gift wrap, greeting cards, tin cans, and even the cover of the Land's End Kids catalog. She lives in Baltimore.

CHARLES BEYL creates humorous illustrations for books, magazines, and newspapers from his studio high atop an old Pennsylvanian farmhouse, surrounded by his family, a cuddly black Labrador, two cats, and three chickens.